THE LEGEND OF PINEAPPLE COVE

A MERMAID'S PROMISE

By **Marina J. Bowman**

Illustrated by **Nathan Monção**

JPF
Bowman

This is a work of fiction. Names, characters, places, and incidents either are the product of the the author's imagination or are used fictitiously. Any resemblance to actual persons, locales, or events, living or dead, is coincidental.

First paperback edition December 2019

Written by Marina J. Bowman
Illustrated by Nathan Monção

ISBN 978-1-950341-11-5 (paperback color)
ISBN 978-1-950341-10-8 (paperback black & white)
ISBN 978-1-950341-09-2 (ebook)

Published by Code Pineapple
www.codepineapple.com

For Don, Paula, Dennis, Jo Anne, Doug, and Morgan.
Wherever you are is home.

ALSO BY MARINA J. BOWMAN

THE LEGEND OF PINEAPPLE COVE

A fantasy-adventure series for kids with bravery, kindness, and friendship. If you like reimagined mythology and animal sidekicks, you'll love this legendary story!

#1 Poseidon's Storm Blaster

#2 A Mermaid's Promise

#3 King of the Sea

#4 Protector's Pledge

SCAREDY BAT

A supernatural detective series for kids with courage, teamwork, and problem solving. If you like solving mysteries and overcoming fears, you'll love this enchanting tale!

#1 Scaredy Bat and the Frozen Vampires

#2 Scaredy Bat and the Sunscreen Snatcher

#3 Scaredy Bat and the Missing Jellyfish

ADVENTURERS

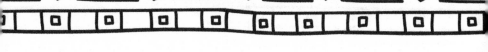

KAI

DELPHI

CAPTAIN HOBBS

AUNT
CORA

CONTENTS

EXTRAS

HIDDEN PINEAPPLE GAME

While you read, keep an eye out for 13 hidden pineapples in the illustrations. When you're finished, you can check the answer key at the back of the book!

There is a place not far from here
Where big adventures await.
It's a town of magic and monsters and secrets
On an island, in the middle of the salty sea.

Pineapple Cove is its name.
The spot where it all begins.

There, kids can be explorers
And ride ships
And follow tattered, dark maps
And become the heroes
They were always meant to be.

CHAPTER 1

THE MOST IMPORTANT JOB

O h, please, please, please can I come with you?" Maya hopped up and down in her seat at the breakfast table.

It was warm and sunny in Kai's house, and Delphi had joined the family for breakfast. Kai's mom had already put out plates for them on the wooden, creaky table. Eggs with runny yolks, sizzling bits of bacon, and delicious fried tomatoes were piled high on the table. He loved it all, and it was the perfect meal for this morning.

Kai and Delphi had their Protector training with Captain Hobbs today.

"Kai, please!" Maya slipped out of her

chair and squeezed between Delphi and Kai. "I know I'm strong enough."

"Sorry, Maya, but you're too young to be a Protector," Kai said.

Delphi nodded between bites of her eggs and bacon. "It can be dangerous. We do obstacle courses and practice cooling down monsters. It's an important job." She puffed out her chest.

Kai's mom sighed. "I hope you two won't give Captain Hobbs any trouble."

"We never give him trouble," Kai said, grinning.

"But sometimes trouble finds us," Delphi added, winking.

It was a joke Kai and Delphi shared, because they had definitely landed in a sticky situation not too long ago. But they had sent away a monster and saved Pineapple Cove. Now, Maya wanted to do the same thing.

"I can be strong," Maya said, lifting her arm. She made a muscle and tapped it. "See? And I can invent things to get rid of monsters!" Maya pointed to a jumble of fishing nets, coconut shells, and bird feathers in the corner of the room.

"Maya, of course you are brilliant and strong," Kai's mom said. "But you're still too young. Maybe when you're a little bit older you can join your brother."

"Hmph." Maya returned to her spot at the table and slumped down in her seat.

"Maya, I would love to see your inventions. Will you show me sometime?" Delphi asked.

"Okay." Maya gave Delphi a small smile.

Kai and Delphi finished off the last bits of their breakfast. Kai loved his sister, even though she could be annoying sometimes. He didn't want her to feel sad about him going off for the day and leaving her behind.

"Maya," he said as he took his plate to the sink. "You can't come with us, but you can do something even more important."

"What?" His sister bounced out of her chair and came over. "I'll do anything."

"You have to make sure you look after Mom while Dad is gone." Kai's dad was a fisherman and was out at sea at the moment. "And make sure that you help her around the house, too."

"That doesn't sound very important." Maya frowned.

"It's the most important job there is. Even more important than training to be a Protector." Kai put his hand on her shoulder. "Do you think you can do that?"

Maya's frown disappeared. Her expression grew serious, and she put her hand up against her forehead. "Yes, sir," she said, and saluted.

Kai gave his sister a quick hug, then did the same with his mom. "I'll be back later!"

"Thanks for breakfast!" said Delphi.

And with that, Kai and Delphi were out the door and on their way to their training.

CHAPTER 2

BANG-SLURP-SQUISH-SLURP

Kai and Delphi walked along the beach together, kicking up clumps of yellow sand. Waves licked their toes and drew back again, showing off pearly shells left behind. The weather was pleasantly warm, as usual.

They both wanted to be Poseidon's Protectors. They had been training almost every day that summer. They would practice their aim with toy water guns, because the Storm Blaster had to be kept safe. They would do puzzles, and Captain Hobbs would teach them about the different types of sea life.

"I can't wait for training today," Delphi said, and dipped her toes in the cool ocean water. The waves rushed over her feet, and Delphi giggled. She was becoming more and more comfortable around water each day.

Sammy the Sea Lion hopped along beside them, barking, his flippers slapping and wet.

"Mm hmm." Kai shrugged.

"What's your favorite part of training?" Delphi asked, twirling her trident necklace.

"I like the obstacle course," Kai said, but he frowned.

"What's wrong?" Delphi asked. "Aren't you excited for training today?" They were on their way to meet Captain Hobbs at Aunt Cora's house. From there, they would head out to their super-secret training spot on the beach.

Kai sighed. "It's just... I already blasted a giant octopus monster, remember?"

"So?"

"So I don't need as much training. I already know how to use the Storm Blaster. It would be more fun to go out exploring and find some real monsters to blast."

"But it's still fun," Delphi said, as they

turned onto the road that led out along the side of the town. The tar was already warm from the heat of the day. "It's nice to feel important. We're Junior Protectors in training. Besides, I like it better than spending all day at home, alone."

Delphi didn't like to be home alone. She didn't have many friends. Lots of the kids in Pineapple Cove thought Delphi was too "different."

"What about Sammy?" Kai asked.

The sea lion barked at Delphi, and she patted him on the head. "Of course, I'm never alone."

But Kai understood what she meant. Delphi had washed up on Pineapple Cove's beach when she was very little. Aunt Cora had adopted her, but Kai knew that Delphi sometimes wondered about where she had come from.

"Are you excited for tonight?" Delphi asked, grinning at him.

They had decided they would have a slumber party. Delphi's Aunt Cora had a house full of interesting sea creatures. Kai couldn't wait to play with them and to stay up late eating coco-nutty cookies.

"It's going to be the best," Kai said. "But what are we going to do?" Hopefully, Delphi wouldn't want to do more sea monster training.

"We can eat sweets. We can play games. And we can explore!"

"Explore?"

"Yeah, in the house. My aunt has a lot of hidden rooms and doors." Delphi rubbed her hands together. "Ooh! And we can tell scary stories."

Kai raised an eyebrow. "What kinds of scary stories?"

Delphi tapped her bottom lip. "Oh, I've got it." She lifted her thin, sticky-outie arms above her head and swirled them around. "And then... it came!"

"What did?" Kai looked at the road ahead.

"The sea monster from the deep, blue ocean."

"Again?" Kai laughed.

"Yes. And it slithered up the sidewalk. It slurped up to the gate. It suckered onto the porch. And then, it reached out one long, slimy leg and BAM!"

Kai jumped and laughed again. Delphi was great at telling stories.

"What did the sea monster do next? Did he break down the village?" Kai patted Sammy on his head.

"No," Delphi replied. "Because he got blasted with a Storm Blaster. He cooled off and went back into the ocean."

Kai frowned. "Why?"

"I don't know," Delphi said. "I think he was under a spell."

Kai had thought the same thing too. The octopus monster had seemed confused after he blasted it. But who would put a spell on a sea monster? And why would they want to hurt Pineapple Cove?

The pair turned and walked back to the road that led past Delphi's house. There had been no more sea monster attacks in two whole weeks. It didn't really matter why the monster had attacked. Did it?

"I think—" Delphi cut off. "What was that noise?"

Kai, Delphi, and Sammy stood still and listened.

BANG-slurp-squish-slurp.

Kai and Delphi turned toward each other with wide eyes. Sammy covered his face with his flippers.

CHAPTER 3

RACE AGAINST SLIME

BANG-sloosh-slurpity-squish.

The sound came again! Was that a... monster?

"Come on," Kai said. "I think there's trouble."

Kai and Delphi took off running toward town. Sammy barked and slapped along behind them.

"Almost there!"

Kai wasn't too worried. After all, he had dealt with one of the horrible sea monsters before. He had used the Storm Blaster to chase it off. If there was another one, Kai would run home, get his blaster and get rid of this one too.

Easy.

Kai rushed past Delphi. He held onto his trident necklace, happy that he had it.

The trio burst into the town square and looked around.

All was quiet. The shops' shutters were closed. Doors were shut, too. Normally, the square was full of townsfolk shopping or talking. The tables outside Kai's favorite restaurant, the Salty Clam, were empty too.

"What's going on?" Delphi asked. "Where is everyone?"

Sammy barked and hopped forward on his flippers.

"There!" Kai called.

A monster slurped into view. It looked like a big blob of green jello, except it had two stalks with bobble eyes on the ends. It left a long trail of oozy green slime behind it. The monster was very quick. It slooshed this way and that way, from shop to shop. A long slimy blob arm reached out and grabbed at the door handles or the windows.

Bang! Slam! Scrabbeldy scrape!

The monster left a trail of broken doors and bits of glass. But it didn't take anything.

What does it want? Kai wondered.

Just then, the monster slithered out of the town square.

"Oh no," Delphi cried. "It's going toward the houses. What do we do?"

"Let's follow it, quick!"

Kai and Delphi set off again and chased after the monster. Kai was determined to protect Pineapple Cove. But what was the monster doing here? Captain Hobbs had told them to prepare, just in case, but Kai had been sure no more would come.

"This way!" Delphi called. "I know a shortcut."

The monster had gone straight down the road. It curled through Pineapple Cove and ended in the streets where all the houses were, apart from Aunt Cora's.

Kai and Delphi, with Sammy flippering after them, turned the corner and ran right across the park. They rushed past the rope swing and the rock slide, taking the dirt path that led out of the park.

They sprinted down the road and reached the street. Kai's house was at the end of the block.

The monster blobbed into sight. He trailed slime up the street and stopped in front of the first house.

"What's he doing?" Delphi asked, grabbing Kai's arm.

"It doesn't matter. Let's go!" He pulled free. They had to get the Storm Blaster before the monster did anything else. If Kai could blast him and get him to cool down, then the monster would go away.

The monster *slurpity-slurped* down the street, past the houses. It was surprisingly fast for a slug-looking thing. It stopped only two times, but Kai didn't care. He raced toward his house. To get to it, he would have to go around the monster.

Before Kai could get close, the monster gooped over the front gate of Kai's house. It squirmed up the path and the steps, then burst through the front door. The walls of the house trembled. The windows at the front broke, and glass fell in the garden. A shocked cry rang out inside.

"Hey, what are you doing?" It was a yell that sounded a lot like Kai's mom.

And then the monster came back out. It held

Kai's mom and his little sister, Maya, under each jelly-ooze arm. It slurped down the steps and across the yard. It was out onto the street in two minutes flat.

"Wait!" Kai raced up the street.

But the jelly monster didn't stop. It carried Kai's mom and sister toward the ocean.

CHAPTER 4

MONSTER MISFIRE

"Quick, after them!" Kai called.

The sea monster had already slithered off down the road. If they could just catch him, Kai could get his mom and sister back. He wasn't afraid. Of course, he wasn't.

Kai set off running after the monster. He followed its oozey green slime trail. It glittered beneath the sun.

"Wait." Delphi caught up to him. She grabbed his arm. "Just wait a second, Kai."

"But it's getting away!"

"We need the Storm Blaster first. Otherwise we can't stop it." Delphi's expression was serious. "You get the Storm Blaster from your hiding spot, and I'll go after the monster. That way, it won't escape."

Kai nodded and ran up to his house. The gate was broken. The path was covered in sticky slime. Kai had to jump from one side of the path to the other.

Finally, he reached the front door. He looked back over his shoulder.

Delphi was already at the end of the street. The monster was out of sight.

"Quickly," Kai muttered. "We can't let it get away!" He was inside at last. The house was usually quite warm, but now, a cold wind rushed through it. Furniture was turned upside down, and the floor was covered in broken bits of wood and glass.

Kai took the stairs two at a time. He ran into his bedroom and flung open his closet doors. He had been hiding the Storm Blaster in there, just in case.

Kai had been sure that no more monsters would come to Pineapple Cove. They would be afraid of Captain Hobbs and of Kai, and of the Storm Blaster, of course.

"Hurry, hurry!" Kai threw his clothes over his shoulders. There went a striped shirt, a pair of shorts. A flip-flop. That one landed on the dresser in the corner. Kai pulled out a round sports ball next. Finally, he found the blaster.

He had hidden it here, in the perfect place. No one would expect to find it under a pile of his clothes and shoes!

He lifted it out and tucked it against his side.

Kai left his bedroom messy and ran down the stairs again. He leaped over the green slime and onto the porch, then down the ruined path and out the rickety gate.

He took off down the road after Delphi and the monster. His heart beat *pit-pat-pit-pat* in his chest.

Kai ran around the outside of the island, following the long trail of slime. Some of it was glittery. All of it was wet. It soaked into the sand and made a dangerous goop. He stepped on a little of it by accident, and it sucked on his foot.

He was caught! Kai yelled and tugged his

foot, but it was no use. He was stuck in the goopy sand!

"Delphi!" he yelled. "Sammy!"

A bark sounded in the distance, and Sammy appeared at the end of the road. He flippered over to Kai.

"Help, Sammy. I'm stuck. The monster's getting away!"

Sammy chomped down on the back of Kai's shirt and pulled.

"Again," Kai yelled.

Sammy tugged a second time, and then a third.

Glop-pop!

Kai's foot popped free. "Yuck!" He shook off the goop. "Quick, Sammy, which way did they go?"

Sammy barked and led Kai down the beach. Delphi was there. She stood in the water, up to her ankles, yelling and throwing small stones. "Hey, you, get back here. You get back here, right now!"

The green goop monster had slurped into the shallow water.

"Stop right there," Kai said, and lifted the Storm Blaster. "From the oceans cold and warm, I summon Poseidon's storm!" He pointed it at the monster and let loose a quick blast of coolness. "Take that!"

But the blast of silvery-blue went wide. It missed the monster completely.

The jelly-ish creature disappeared beneath the waves, taking Kai's mom and little sister with it.

"Try again," Delphi shouted.

But it was too late. They were gone.

Kai gripped the Storm Blaster and stared at the waves, the beautiful blue ocean. The monster had left bubbles behind—maybe they could chase it?

Delphi nudged Kai. "Come on, we have to get Captain Hobbs. He'll know what to do."

CHAPTER 5

THE HIDDEN MESSAGE

T his way," Delphi said. "Captain Hobbs is waiting at my aunt Cora's house, remember?"

Together, Delphi, Kai and Sammy tore off across the sand. They had to dodge the slime trail the monster had left behind. Some of the green goop had dried a bit, now. Kai was slower than usual. He was a pretty good runner, but he couldn't stop thinking about what had happened.

He had missed the shot! Why? He was able to blast the giant octopus monster before... Why did he miss the green blob monster today? Maybe he needed the training with Captain Hobbs, after all. But it was too late to worry about that. Kai's mom and sister were gone. Kai wouldn't let the monster get away with it. He would bring his family back.

"Hey, what's that?" Delphi asked.

"What?"

Delphi pointed at a slip of paper stuck in the slime on the sand. "There, see? What do you think it could be?"

Kai and Delphi slowed down. The slime was almost as hard as a rock now.

"It's a note. Hey, and it has your name on it!" Delphi said.

They tried pulling it out, but the goop was too hard. "What do we do?" Kai asked. "We have to get it out of this gross gunk."

A muffled bark sounded behind them.

"Oh, of course!" Delphi shouted. "Sammy, you're a genius."

The sea lion held Kai's big red clam bucket in his mouth. He often left it behind on the beach, tucked behind their favorite rocky spot to sit. Kai and Delphi loved collecting fresh clams in the bucket together.

Now, it was empty.

"We can fill this with water." Delphi suggested. "Maybe if we make the slime wet again, we can get the note out." She hurried to the water and filled the bucket, then brought it back.

Together, they poured the water onto the goo, carefully.

"I'll get the note," Delphi said.

She held onto the end of it as the goo loosened. Finally, she pulled the note free and held it upright. "Got it!"

"Great!" Kai dumped the rest of the water onto the goop, then walked his bucket back to the rocks. He tucked it into his hiding spot. "What does it say?"

Delphi had gone pale. It was strange for her to look pale at all—she was very tan from lots of time in the sun. "Come look at this." She held out the note.

Kai took it from her and read out loud, "Dear Kai. We have taken your mom and sister. You must hand over the Storm Blaster within twenty-four hours or we will keep them forever!" The note wasn't signed, and the bottom part was torn off. But there was a strange blue liquid on it. It had dried on the paper.

Kai's heart was beating fast. "Well, at least we know my family is safe, for now." He looked down at the note again. "But it doesn't say where we're supposed to go!"

"Oh no! What do we do?" Delphi pressed her hands over her mouth.

"Maybe Captain Hobbs can figure this out?" Kai hoped so. Otherwise, they would never be able to find his mom and sister. But they couldn't give up the Storm Blaster either. It was meant for a Protector. "Come on, Delphi. We need to get to Aunt Cora's house, right away."

They hurried into town. Lots of people had already come out of their houses to look at the damage. It wasn't too bad. Some of the roof shingles hung loose or bricks were broken. The florist's shop sign hung sideways and creaked in the wind. The baker's shop had a broken window, and bread loaves spilled out onto the road. The streets were missing a few stones here and there, as well. The air smelled of fresh, salty sea. Still, the people of the town were upset.

A monster attack, again?

Kai and Delphi had to run past all of them in the town square. They didn't answer any questions. They took their favorite shortcut across the park, then onto the road that led along the beach and right up to Aunt Cora's house.

The house looked just as Kai remembered it, complete with a front porch and seashell stepping-stone path. It was rickety and twisty, and three stories high. It reminded Kai of magic. And now, he knew magic *could* be real.

They went inside and found Captain Hobbs sitting at the dining room table, enjoying a refreshing piña pop. He smiled at them as they entered.

"Captain Hobbs, we need your help!" Kai announced. "A monster has attacked the Cove, a big, green, blobby one, and it took my family."

Delphi handed over the note. "Here, look at this, Captain."

Captain Hobbs read it quickly, his bushy eyebrows lifting and falling in time with his reading. "This isn't good."

"What are we going to do? Who do you think left the note?" Kai asked.

"I'm not sure yet. But what's this?" Captain

Hobbs pointed to the blue stain on the paper. "Slime, hmmm. We need to figure out which creature made it. Then we can find out where it came from. I bet your aunt knows more about this."

"That's a great idea," Delphi said. "Aunt Cora knows just about every animal in the sea."

Captain Hobbs rose from his seat. "Come on, Kai. Let's go talk to Cora. We'll get your mom and sister back, don't worry."

CHAPTER 6

I HAVE AN IDEA

Kai, Delphi, and Captain Hobbs left the dining room to find Aunt Cora.

"She said she was going upstairs to do some painting," Captain Hobbs said.

"Oh! I know the way." Delphi led the group up the rickety stairs, past the cages and wonderful tanks full of bubble-blowing fish and tiny seahorses. Kai waved at Finley, and the fish flapped his fin at Kai. Finley smiled his wicked, toothy smile, and Kai grinned back. They reached the second floor of the house and made their way down a long, curving passage.

"This house is huge." Kai peered around once they reached the third floor. He had never been up here before. It seemed impossible that the house could be this big inside.

Sparkly pictures in wooden frames decorated the walls, mostly of painted sea creatures or old, worn maps.

Finally, Delphi knocked on a hardwood door at the end of the passage.

The door opened. Aunt Cora was full of smiles as usual, but soon a big frown turned her lips down at the corners. Kai and Delphi told her all about the green blob monster and how it had taken Kai's mom and sister.

"It was a different monster than last time!" said Delphi.

"We couldn't stop it." Kai bowed his head.

"Oh, you poor dears," Aunt Cora said. "Let's go downstairs and I'll make us some tea. It always helps me see things more clearly." She put her hand on Kai's shoulder. "Together we'll come up with a plan to get your family back."

They followed Aunt Cora back down the twisty stairs and into the kitchen, past the amazing creatures and tanks and cages. The kitchen had charming seashell counters and smelled of coconut.

In no time, they had their tea and coco-nutty cookies and were telling Aunt Cora about the ransom note.

Kai loved Aunt Cora's cookies, but he didn't have much of an appetite. He took the ransom note out and put it on the table. "Look, Aunt Cora, it's got this strange blue ink all over it. Do you know what it is? Or where it comes from?"

"Let me see." Aunt Cora lifted the note and placed it right against her nose. She sniffed the stain, turned the note upside down and the right way around. Her large hazel eyes twinkled and narrowed. "Sirenia Orbis."

"Huh?" Kai saw from Delphi's blank stare that she was as confused as he was.

"It comes from Sirenia Orbis: the Mermaid World," Aunt Cora clarified.

Delphi gasped. "Mermaid World?"

"How do you know?" Kai perked up.

"This gel comes from a special type of blue

jellyfish, also known as the 'dancing jelly.' It lives very far underwater, and it only comes to the surface once a year, right near the entrance to the Mermaid World. The monster must have come from the place where the jellyfish live."

Delphi stared at her aunt with wide eyes. "But how do we get there?"

Captain Hobbs winked at them. "Leave that to me."

Delphi squirmed in her seat. "Oh, this is so exciting. We know where to find Kai's family! *And* we get to explore a whole new world. Oh please, Aunt Cora, can I go? I need to help Kai find his mom and Maya."

Aunt Cora screwed up her lips like she'd tasted a lemon.

"Don't worry," Captain Hobbs said. "I'll be with them every step of the way. I know how to get into Sirenia."

"All right." Aunt Cora took a bite of her crumbly cookie. "But what are you going to do about the Storm Blaster?"

"I have an idea." The Captain scratched his bushy beard. "I have a few merpeople friends. One of them is a master blacksmith and owes me a favor. I bet, if I find him, he'll make a copy of the Storm Blaster for us."

"But Captain Hobbs, how does that help?" Kai asked. "Will we have two blasters to use then?"

"Well, if we have a copy of the Storm Blaster, we can hide the real one, and trade the fake one for your mom and sister. The copied Storm Blaster won't be infused with Poseidon's power, so it won't work. And the true Storm Blaster won't fall into the wrong hands."

Kai liked that idea. This way, he would get his family back *and* keep the Storm Blaster.

Suddenly the dining table started to rumble and shake. Kai jumped backward. "What is that?!"

"Is it an earthquake?"

"Is it a monster?"

Delphi burst out laughing and pointed under the table. Kai leaned down and saw Sammy lying on the floor, snoring.

Everyone relaxed, and Captain Hobbs continued sharing his plan.

"My merman friend probably knows where those jellyfish live too. We could find the kidnappers before they even know we're coming!" Captain Hobbs clapped his big hands together and rubbed them. "Yes, that should work just fine. Are you ready, kids?"

Kai grabbed his trident necklace and held it tight. "I'm ready. Let's go!"

CHAPTER 7

SIRENIA ORBIS

The group boarded Captain Hobbs' ship just before sunset. The waves splashed against the side of the boat as they sailed. The sky was clear, but turning a deep orange. Seagulls cawed overhead.

Aunt Cora refused to join them on their journey, but she wouldn't explain why.

Kai gripped the Storm Blaster and stood near the wheel. A strange wooden lever poked out next to it. Kai reached out to pull it.

"Don't touch that!" warned Captain Hobbs.

"Why? What does it do?" asked Kai.

"Never you mind that now; we're almost there." The captain steered them toward the magical rock archway that was actually a portal. It was the same one they had used to get to Poseidon's Island.

"This is the same place as last time." Delphi patted Sammy's blubbery head.

"Yes, we're going to use the portal to get to the Mermaid World." Captain Hobbs pointed at Kai and Delphi. "You two must go to the front of the ship and say, 'by Poseidon's will, take us to Sirenia Orbis,' and then it will open up for us."

Kai and Delphi hurried to the prow of the boat. They held out their trident necklaces. "By Poseidon's will, take us to Sirenia Orbis."

The gap between the stones of the archway shimmered. There was a bright pink-blue flash. And then, the portal showed a view of the other side. A bright sunny day, and a white sandy beach. On the beach, there was a long dock, and a set of steps that led into the water.

Two merpeople guards floated in the water next to it. They wore their hair in long braids. They flipped their shimmery tails, dove under the water and came back out again.

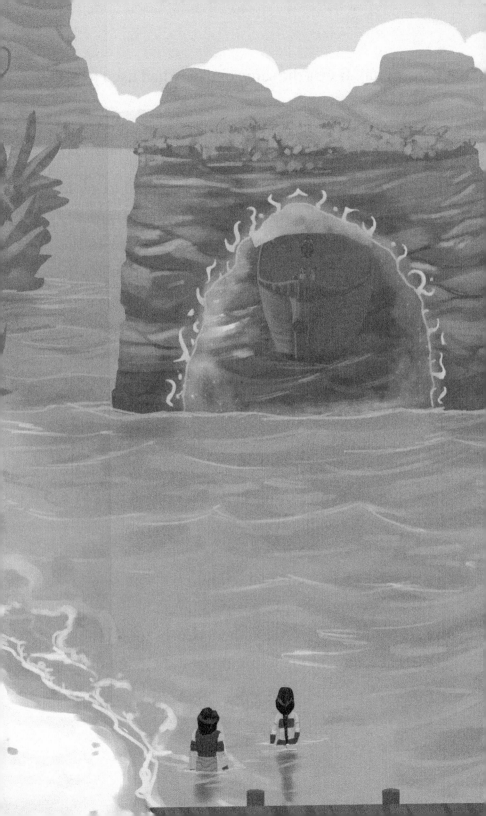

"Here we go!" Captain Hobbs called out. "Everyone hold on to something."

Kai grabbed hold of the railing and tucked the Storm Blaster against his chest.

Quick as could be, the captain sailed them underneath the archway's glimmering rocks and into the sunny waters on the other side.

"It's morning here!" Delphi cried.

"It's the magic of Sirenia," Captain Hobbs replied. "It's always morning here." He steered their ship to the dock. Kai and Delphi dropped the anchor and let down the gangplank.

"Who goes there?" The merman guard lifted himself out of the water. He leaned against the steps.

"Captain Hobbs." The captain gave a salute. "And this is Kai and Delphi."

Sammy barked twice. "And this is Sammy."

Delphi's eyes were round. "Look at their beautiful blue tails," she whispered.

"I'm here to speak with Hermes," the captain continued. "He can vouch for us."

"Hermes?" The guards looked at each other.

The female guard nodded. "Wait right here. We'll find him." And then they disappeared beneath the surf.

"The Mermaid World is down there?" Delphi asked, rising on her tiptoes. She peered into the water. "How are we going to breathe?"

"Don't worry," Captain Hobbs said. "Hermes can help with that."

Kai licked his lips. He was itching to get down there and find out what was really going on.

Luckily, they didn't have to wait very long.

Hermes erupted out of the water and flashed a golden-scaled tail. He had a friendly face and dark skin and eyes. He held three helmets in his strong hands. "Captain Hobbs!" He laughed. "It's wonderful to see you. I never thought we would meet at the entrance to my world."

"It's good to see you too, Hermes. I wish it were under better circumstances," Captain Hobbs said. "Kai here needs help."

"Hobbs, you know I'll do whatever I can to help you. Do you need to come down into Sirenia?" Hermes asked.

"Yes, please," Delphi squeaked. Her cheeks were flushed. She was very excited about meeting a real-life merman.

"Take these." Hermes flipped the helmets at them one at a time, using his sparkly tail. "They will help you breathe underwater."

"Thank you," the three said together.

The helmet was made of a special glass or crystal. It had gills along the side. Kai put it on and took a deep breath. It was lovely, fresh air.

"What about Sammy?" Delphi asked. "He can only hold his breath for twenty minutes. That's not long enough, is it?"

Hermes raised an eyebrow at his friend, and Captain Hobbs shrugged.

"Of course, I will return in a moment." Hermes dove back into the water, and after a few minutes he returned with a fourth helmet. He handed it to Delphi, and she squeezed it onto Sammy's head.

"Is there anything else I can do?" Hermes asked.

"We also need you to take this and make a copy of it," the Captain whispered, pointing to the Storm Blaster. "But it's very important that nobody else know about this. Can you do that, Hermes?"

"Of course, Captain. You saved my family. You can count on me."

Kai came forward and handed the Storm

Blaster to Hermes. It felt very strange to give it away.

"Good," the captain said. "Then we'll follow you down. Are you ready?"

"I am!" Delphi said.

Kai couldn't stand still a moment longer. He dove into the crystal blue water. Bubbles tickled past his ears as he followed Hermes down into the depths.

CHAPTER 8

AN UNEXPECTED VISITOR

The water was warm, and Kai, Delphi and the captain followed Hermes down, lower and lower. It was easy swimming. Currents carried them, so they didn't have to kick their legs much. The deeper they swam, the colder it got – goosebumps prickled on Kai's arms.

Just when Kai thought it couldn't possibly get any colder, a warm current swished over them. Delphi bumped against him. She was looking up toward the surface of the water.

"I didn't think it would be this far down," Delphi said, twisting her hands.

"You can do this, Delphi. You're almost a better swimmer than me now!" Kai squeezed her hand.

Hermes looped back toward them. "We're almost there," he said.

Delphi nodded, and they continued swimming.

Very soon, they found a forest of green kelp, swaying in the aquamarine water. Between the long stalks, blue and pink lights glowed. They were big see-through shells, glimmering on top of sticks.

Delphi gasped and pointed at them, and Kai laughed. At least Delphi was happy. Kai couldn't help worrying about his mom and sister. But Captain Hobbs seemed to know what was going on, and that made him feel a little better.

They made it through the forest of seaweed and followed the lights, lower and lower. Bubbles *blurped* out of the sides of their helmets.

Buildings and beautiful seashell domes

appeared underneath. There seemed to be a lot of merpeople swimming around the opening to a huge arena. It was full of glistening stone steps to sit on, and in the very center, there was a racetrack. It had seaweed too, but it was much shorter.

"What's that?" Delphi asked, her voice filled with wonder.

"That's the seahorse race." Hermes lowered his voice. "You three wait here while I go make a copy of the blaster. I'll be back in no time."

"Thank you, Hermes," Captain Hobbs said.

The merman split off from the group, speeding away into the water. He was an incredible swimmer with that golden tail.

Captain Hobbs led Kai and Delphi down into the stands. They didn't have to pay anything to sit and watch the races. But Kai could hardly sit still. He wanted to run off and find his family, not sit and watch seahorses race around the track.

"Isn't it amazing?" Delphi asked. "Look at them go!"

They were the biggest seahorses Kai had ever seen, much bigger than the tiny ones at Aunt Cora's house. The creatures were pink or blue or purple or green or… so many other colors. They shimmered as they swept through the water, their eyes narrowed. Merpeople riders clung to their reins but didn't sit on saddles.

"Do you like it?" Another mermaid, who had a long, swishy pink tail and glossy pink hair, smiled at Delphi. "We have seahorse races once a week. They're my favorite!"

"You're so lucky!" Delphi exclaimed. "We only have normal, people races in Pineapple Cove."

"I'm Lily. What's your name?" asked the mermaid.

"I'm Delphi, and this is Sammy," Delphi said.

"It's very nice to meet you." Lily scratched under Sammy's chin. The sea lion made a gurgling purr sound, and Delphi giggled.

Kai folded his arms. He shifted on the spot and looked around. Maybe he could swim off and find the special blue jellyfish by himself?

"Are you all right, Kai?" Captain Hobbs asked.

"I want to get going."

"We have to be patient. We can't do anything without the Storm Blaster," the captain whispered. Cheers rose up around them as another seahorse race started.

"Right, the Storm Blaster." Kai slumped down in the stands. The last time he had used it, he had missed! If he had hit the green blob monster with a cooling blast, they wouldn't even be here.

The time passed too slowly for Kai's liking.

The races were lively, but Kai didn't enjoy them as much as Delphi. She and the pink-haired mermaid chatted away, laughing and joking. Delphi looked happier than Kai had ever seen her.

Just then, a squeaky cry rang out, and Blue the Dolphin appeared. He was a flash of blueish-gray. He stopped in front of Captain Hobbs and nudged him.

"What is it, Blue?" the captain asked.

"What?" He untied a kelp scroll from the dolphin's fin and unrolled the message. The captain's jaw dropped. "Mother of Pearl!"

"What's wrong?" Kai asked.

"A very important artifact has been stolen: a crystal egg. It's very powerful. In the wrong hands..." Captain Hobbs trailed off. "It's my duty to protect it. Well, it used to be, anyway."

"Then you should go find it, right?" Kai asked.

"Not until we've found your family and I know you're safe. I won't leave you two alone." The captain looked around at Delphi and her new mermaid friend. "We need to, well, you know... find the jellyfish."

"The jellyfish?" Lily asked.

"Yes, we're looking for a very specific type of glittery blue jellyfish," Delphi replied.

"Oh! I know where they live. They're near a cave west of Sirenia City, just past the Kelp Forest." Lily smiled. "I would take you there myself, but it's time I returned home. I hope to see you again soon." The mermaid winked at Delphi and swished her tail, leaving the stadium behind.

Kai leaped to his feet. "All right, let's go."

"No, Kai," Captain Hobbs said. "Remember, don't be hasty. We have to get the… you know, first." He spoke softly so that none of the other mermaids on the fancy benches would hear. "Hermes should be back any minute—well, speak of the devil!"

Hermes joined them with the blaster in hand. "I ran into a little trouble, but nothing we can't – hey, what's Blue doing here?"

The dolphin chirped happily as Hermes patted him on the head.

Captain Hobbs told him the news of the missing crystal egg. Hermes' mouth fell open. "This is terrible! You must go after it, Hobbs, immediately."

Captain Hobbs shook his head. "I won't leave Kai and Delphi alone. I need to help Kai save his family."

"It's okay, Captain. Hermes can help us. You should go," said Kai.

"Yeah, we'll be safe with Hermes! He probably knows Sirenia Orbis even better than you!" Delphi chimed in.

Worry lines crinkled Captain Hobbs' forehead. "Are you sure you'll be okay without me?"

"Yes!" Delphi and Kai said together.

"I'll take good care of them, Hobbs," said Hermes. "Now go."

"Alright, be safe. I'll be back before you know it." Captain Hobbs took hold of Blue's fin, and the dolphin swam him away.

CHAPTER 9

THE COLLECTOR

Now, about the Storm Blaster..." said Hermes. The seahorse races had ended, and swarms of mermaids were leaving the stadium. Kai and Delphi looked down at the single blaster in Hermes' hands.

"Why do you only have one blaster?" Kai asked.

Hermes held it out. "This is the copy," he said. "But we have a problem. The Collector took the original."

"Who's the Collector?" Delphi asked, patting Sammy on his head. He gave a concerned *arf.*

Hermes explained it to them quickly. "The Collector is an old squid that collects everything he can get his tentacles on. He's the one who has the copy maker. So, I went to his mansion to copy the Storm Blaster, but right after I made the copy, his guards found me and threw me out. He took the original Storm Blaster!"

"Oh no," Delphi said. "What do we do now?"

Hermes put two fingers between his lips and whistled loudly. Three merpeople appeared, with three seahorses between them. "Here. These seahorses will take us to the Collector's mansion. From there we'll head to the caves west of Sirenia City to find the blue jellyfish."

Delphi squealed and clapped her hands at the sight of the seahorses. She hurried over to one of the creatures.

Kai was relieved—no more waiting around. They were finally on their way to find his family. He looked from the seahorses to the blaster in Hermes' hands. Kai frowned. Once they got the original back and found his family, would he actually be able to save them?

"Don't worry," Hermes said to Kai. "They're well trained."

"I'm not worried. Well, not about the seahorses," Kai said.

Hermes looked at Kai with wise brown eyes. "You know, when I was first learning to be a blacksmith, I was the top of my class. Everything came easy to me. I could make lengths of chain that went on forever before others could finish a few links."

"Really?" Kai knew very little about the merman.

"Yes, really. But soon I became overconfident and bored, so I stopped practicing. One day, I was asked to build a sculpture for the Queen of Sirenia. I tried my best, but could not finish it in time. It was then that I realized something very important."

"What did you realize?" asked Kai.

"Natural talent can only get us so far. Patience and practice are how we accomplish great things." Hermes held out the copied blaster to Kai. "Now, let's go get the Storm Blaster and save your family." Kai took the copy from him and nodded.

Hermes helped them get on the seahorses. Delphi's was pink with yellow stripes, and Kai's was a deep sea green. Hermes' seahorse was the biggest of them all, and a lovely purplish-blue.

Kai slipped and nearly fell off his a few times, but Delphi seemed just fine. She sat

straight and stroked her seahorse's neck. It made a strange purring noise and leaned its head against her hand.

"Hang on tight to the reins. They go very fast," Hermes told them.

"Keep up, Sammy," Delphi said over her shoulder to her sea lion friend.

And then they were off.

The seahorses zipped through the water so fast, Kai's stomach did a loop-de-loop. Delphi shrieked and giggled. Sammy flippered through the water, following closely behind.

They swept over the gorgeous mermaid city below, then through streets with shell walkways. The windows of shell houses had glass that shimmered in a rainbow of colors. It was all so beautiful.

Some of the houses had long, clear chimneys that made bubbles. Each time a bubble popped out, it went *bloop*, and Kai and Delphi would giggle.

"This place is… It feels right," Delphi said.

"What do you mean?" Kai asked. They sped down the street, past mermaids who smiled at them.

"I don't know. It seems like everyone here is friendly. No one has teased me or told me that I'm weird. And Lily was so nice. She told me all about Sirenia City and the seahorse races every week. I wish I could race seahorses."

"It's nice here," Kai agreed. "But I miss Pineapple Cove."

"I don't," Delphi said. "Not that much."

Kai opened his mouth to ask why, but Delphi swung behind him as they passed between two 'blooping' houses. Bubbles bounced off their helmets and popped noiselessly.

The further they went, the quieter it became. The seahorses brought them outside the mermaid city and through a kelp forest with swishing leaves.

Finally, the seahorses slowed. They swept toward a strange-looking wall made out of stone and dirt. Then they swished over it, and Kai gasped. Delphi did too.

A palace lay in front of them, if it could be called that.

It was higgledy piggledy, made out of stones and bits of broken seashells. Some of its rooms seemed to have been glued on crooked, and still others were connected to it by thin bridges of kelp rope.

"Down here." Hermes led them down to one side of the palace. He slid off his purple seahorse, and Kai and Delphi did the same.

"The Collector has the Storm Blaster inside," Hermes told them.

Kai wanted to run inside right away but stopped himself. He remembered what Hermes had told him. "So, what's the plan?" asked Kai.

"You two will have to sneak in," Hermes whispered. "I can't go back because they know what I look like, but they don't know you. They might think you are friends of the Collector, since he has so many strange friends."

"How do we get in?" Delphi asked.

Hermes showed them the open windows near the kelp rope on the side of the palace. "There. You will have to sneak down the hall and find the Blaster. Good luck."

CHAPTER 10

A TRADE OF JEWELS & JUNK

Kai and Delphi swam up to the window together. Kai held the copied Storm Blaster to his chest.

The closer they got, the harder and faster Kai's heart beat. They had been in the Mermaid World for a long time now. Which meant Maya and his mom had been there even longer. What if they didn't have the breathing helmets like Kai and Delphi did?

Kai was itchy all over to run off and find them.

"In here," Delphi whispered.

They entered a lopsided window that didn't have any glass. A long passageway with a dirt floor and shimmery seashell walls lay in front of them. There were doorways that led off into different rooms on either side.

"What now?" Delphi asked. "How are we supposed to find the Collector?"

Kai shrugged and set off. He had to be in here somewhere. They hurried down the hallway, checking each room. A lot of them had piles of gold or silver coins, glowing jewels and crowns, and others had garbage, like shiny chipped seashells or bottles. The Collector seemed to like all of it, and he put the gold jewels and cases next to the bottles and caps.

Delphi and Kai wandered down the hall.

Footsteps stomped toward them, and a pair of guards rounded the far corner.

"Hey!" one of them said. "What are you doing here?" He had tentacles where his mouth should have been, and a big mustache. He pointed his spear. "Intruders."

"No, we're not intruders," Delphi said quickly. "We're here to see the Collector. We have a special gift for him." She pointed to the copied Storm Blaster in Kai's arms.

"Oh. All right. This way." The guards marched them down the hallway and into a grand room.

The Collector floated above a throne made out of glassy seashells. He clutched the real Storm Blaster in his tentacles. "What's this?" he asked. "Another back scratcher?"

Kai and Delphi looked at each other. The

Collector thought the Storm Blaster was a back scratcher?

"Yes," Delphi said. "You have to give us that one because it's actually... um. It's..." She didn't seem to know what else to say.

"That Blas--I mean, back scratcher doesn't work properly," Kai said. "Here, I can show you the difference."

Kai walked up to the Collector. "May I show you?" he asked.

"Yes." The Collector's voice was wet and wobbly, and his beady black eyes focused on Kai.

Kai pumped the handle on the copied Blaster. "See? This back scratcher releases bubbles that feel great on the skin. The one you have doesn't do that. Let me show you." Kai reached for the blaster.

"No!" The Collector gripped the real Storm Blaster to his chest. "This one is mine!"

Delphi bit her lip.

Kai's stomach grew nervous and squirmy.

The guards stood in the doorway and watched them closely.

What now?

"All right," Kai said. "You can see for yourself. Just pump the handle like this and see what happens." Kai motioned with the copied Blaster, and the Collector did the same. He pointed the real Blaster at his squiddy face. "Now, pump the handle here," Kai instructed.

The Collector pumped the handle on the Blaster. Nothing happened. He tried again and still nothing. "Argh, it's broken!" He looked greedily at the blaster in Kai's hands. "Okay, I'll trade you."

Kai and the Collector swapped blasters. As Kai turned and began to walk away, the Collector spoke again. "On second thought, I'll take both. Guards!"

"Blast him, Kai!" Delphi shouted.

Kai spun around and quickly muttered the words: "From the oceans cold and warm, I summon Poseidon's storm." Kai aimed the blaster at the Collector, and a cool blast of white hit him in the face. Immediately, he dropped the copy.

"Got it!" Delphi shouted as she scooped up the blaster.

"Get them!" one of the guards yelled.

Delphi grabbed Kai by the arm and pointed to the window behind the Collector's throne. The big old squid floated around, shaking his head and muttering. He couldn't understand what had happened.

Quickly, Kai and Delphi swam out of the window and past the kelp ropes, down to the waiting Hermes and Sammy.

"We did it!" shouted Delphi. "Kai blasted the Collector! We have both the original and copy."

"Well done," Hermes said. "You'd better get out of here, now. I'll keep the guards busy and join you in a moment."

"Which way is the cave west of Sirenia City?" Kai asked as they mounted their seahorses again.

"It's that way," Hermes said, and pointed.

A yell sounded from the front of the palace, and five guards ran out. They held ropes and chains in their hands.

"Go, quickly!" Hermes cried.

Delphi and Kai jumped onto their sea horses and sped away, with Sammy following closely behind.

CHAPTER 11

THE DANCING JELLY

The trip through the kelp forest was very tickly. The seaweed was soft and brushed against Kai's arms and face. He didn't laugh, though. He couldn't stop worrying about Maya and his mom. He did feel better about his ability to use the Storm Blaster now.

Finally, they made it through the forest and stopped in front of the entrance to a cave. It was blocked by a door, which was covered in glittery blue jellyfish.

"I think this is the place," Delphi said, letting go of the reins of the seahorse. It stayed where she left it.

The cave was surrounded by bright yellow seaweed. It swayed from side to side, and blue jellyfish drifted past.

"We'll have to pull the jellyfish off the door," Kai said.

Sammy nudged one of the jellyfish with his nose. It let out a puff of glittery goo, and Sammy whined and shook his nose.

Delphi got a closer look at the door. "No, Kai, I think they're stuck to it. And we can't touch the jellyfish without getting stung." She sighed inside her waterproof helmet. "I don't think we will be able to get inside without getting them free."

Kai chewed on the inside of his cheek. But how could they do that? He stared at the graceful creatures, moving to their own rhythm.

"Oh, I have an idea!" Delphi exclaimed. "We should sing them a song!"

"Huh?" Kai was totally confused.

"Remember what Aunt Cora said? About how this type of jellyfish is known as the dancing jelly?" Delphi asked.

It finally hit Kai. "Oh, yeah!" He closed his eyes and thought for a moment. "I know a song... My mom taught it to Maya and me."

Delphi nodded. "Let's try it."

Kai started out softly and then sang louder as the words came back to him.

> *Oh the sea, the ocean, the ocean, the sea*
> *It all means the very same thing to me*
> *The sea, the ocean, the ocean, the sea*
> *I live on land but the sea is for me*

When I was a babe, my dad said to me
The ocean's a treasure, rare as can be
Just hear me, my dear, oh, listen to me
The greatest treasure, beautiful sea

"It's working!" Delphi whispered. "Keep singing, Kai."

Sure enough, the jellyfish began floating away from the door, swishing their bodies back and forth. Delphi joined Kai in the singing, and even more jellyfish started dancing. Kai never knew she had such a nice singing voice. Sammy joined in too, with an *arf* here and an *arf* there.

When I was five, my dad said to me
The call of the deep is a mystery
You cannot resist the stormy plea
The deep blue magic, beautiful sea

When I was ten, my dad said to me
The creatures so deep are family
I wish I had gills so I could swim free
With creatures so deep, beautiful sea

And now I'm all grown, with little ones wee,
I tell them their mother is the sea
She gives food and water, all that is key
Mother to us all, beautiful sea

Soon the last of the jellyfish had detached from the door. They swirled from side to side, up and down. Kai stopped singing and grinned. They'd done it. He handed the Storm Blaster to Delphi to hold, and she hid it under her shirt.

Kai had the copy, and Delphi had the real Blaster. The kidnapper wouldn't expect them to have two, and he wouldn't expect Delphi to blast them. Kai was nervous, but ready. Nothing would stop him from getting his family back!

They moved toward the opening. But, oh no! It wasn't open at all.

It was still blocked by a stone door, covered in strange squiggly markings.

"How do we open the door?" Kai asked.

"That's easy," Delphi said. "It's a riddle."

"Wait, you can read that?" Kai asked. "But

it looks like… a different language."

"Yes, I can read it. Hold on a minute." Delphi squinted at the squiggly writing. "It says, 'What is hard but soft, glitters like a gem in the sun, and is priceless to its owner but has no value?"

Kai blinked. He had no idea. He wasn't very good at puzzles. "Um? A Jellyfish?"

The door didn't budge.

"A star?" He guessed again.

Still, the door didn't open. What would they do now? What if they couldn't get inside?

Kai looked over at Delphi. She was staring at a school of fish that were swimming past, moving this way and that. Sammy looked at the fish too and licked his lips.

"I've got it," Delphi said, and raised her finger. "It's scales. Fish scales."

The door gave a terrific rumble. It swung open and showed the long, dark passage beyond.

CHAPTER 12

QUEEN OF SIRENIA

The corridor was dark, and a little bit frightening. Colorful lights glowed farther down the hallway, pink and blue like they had seen in the Kelp Forest.

Kai took a deep breath and stepped into the hall, holding his fake Blaster. It wouldn't work, but it was nice to carry it and pretend.

The door slammed shut behind them, and Delphi let out a cry. "It's closing! What do we do?"

Just then, two monsters slurped into view. One was the green blob monster who had taken Kai's family! The other was purple, with one giant eye in the center of its head.

"Hey, where's my family?" Kai asked, pointing the Blaster.

The monsters grabbed hold of Kai, Delphi, and Sammy and brought them down the corridor. Kai didn't struggle. Still, it was scary. They would finally meet the horrible monster who had written the note.

What would he look like? Ugly and brown and…

They were brought into a wide chamber. On the edges, yellow seaweed swished and glowed in the water. Monsters stood between the kelp fronds. There were many different colors, shapes and sizes of monsters, and between them all floated mermaids!

"There you are." A beautiful mermaid with long, pink hair and a matching tail sat on top of a throne at the end of the room. "It took you long enough to find me."

Kai was shocked. It was Lily from the seahorse races.

"No!" Delphi said. "Lily? What on earth are you doing here?"

"My name isn't Lily, you silly girl. I'm Amphi, Queen of Sirenia Orbis. I knew you had the Storm Blaster all along, because my fish have been watching you from shore."

Amphi swam off the throne. "And I'm the one who took your family. Bob! Bring them out."

The green gloopy monster slurped into view. Bob held Kai's mom and sister under either arm. They had on helmets to help them breathe too. They didn't seem hurt, but Maya's eyes darted around like she was looking for an escape.

"Give me my family back," Kai demanded. He was relieved that they were safe. Now was the time to act. He raised the fake Blaster and aimed it. "If you don't, I'll have to give you a blast." It was all part of the act. Amphi had no idea that his blaster didn't work.

"Not so fast," Amphi replied with a swish of her tail. "If you blast me, you will never get your family back. You must hand over the Storm Blaster, now. Give it to me."

"Why are you doing this?" Delphi asked. "Why do you want the Storm Blaster? It's not meant for you. It's for Poseidon's Protectors."

"You know why. You and Kai have been talking to Poseidon. You are his favorites!"

Amphi pouted. "He never visits me anymore. Once I have the Storm Blaster, he will finally come see me to retrieve it." Amphi pointed at Kai, then waved to his mom and sister. "Hand it over, or you will never see your family again."

Kai's heart skipped a few beats. It was time for them to put their master plan into action. The only problem was, they hadn't expected to use the Blaster on a mermaid. Would it cool her down the same way it had cooled down the octopus monster?

He looked over at Delphi, who nodded.

"That's right." Amphi swished forward, waving her tail from side to side. She put out a hand. "Come. Give the Blaster to me." She paused. "Bob, bring the prisoners forward."

All around the inside of the lair, the monsters and mermaids watched. Some of them had come a little closer. They probably thought he would fire the Blaster.

Kai took one step forward and then another. He lifted the copied Storm Blaster and held it out.

CHAPTER 13

A SECRET REVEALED

Kai's mom and sister hurried forward. Finally, they were next to Kai, and then behind him and safe with Delphi. Sammy flopped in front of them, puffed out his chest, and barked loudly.

"Here," Kai said, holding up the fake blaster. "Take it."

"A-ha!" Amphi cried, grabbing the copied Storm Blaster. She pointed it at them. "Now, you're going to tell me where—"

"Now, Delphi!" Kai yelled.

Quickly, Delphi drew the real Storm Blaster out from under her shirt. She lifted it and pumped the handle. Nothing happened. She tried again, and still nothing happened.

Delphi looked over at Kai with wide eyes. "Why isn't it working?"

Then Kai remembered. "The words! You have to say the words!"

"Oh, right!" Delphi said. "From the oceans cold and warm, I summon Poseidon's storm!" The blaster glowed, and a long blast of cool blue-white shot out of its end. It struck Amphi right in the chest.

Amphi closed her eyes and shook her head. Her expression went from an angry frown to calm and peaceful.

Delphi blasted the other mermaids and monsters who came forward, and each time, the anger washed away. They were, finally, all calm.

"Oh my," Amphi said, and dropped the fake Blaster. She pressed her hand against her forehead. "Oh my goodness."

"Please, let my friends and family leave," Kai said.

Amphi nodded. "Of course, of course. I'm so sorry. I wasn't thinking straight. I was just so upset because I haven't heard from Poseidon in quite a while. I thought he was ignoring me. I thought if I had the Storm Blaster, I could get him to pay attention to me again. That's what a friend told me, anyway…"

"We haven't heard from him either," Delphi said, helpfully.

Kai's mom and sister rushed over to him. Kai's mom gave him a big hug and a mushy kiss on the cheek. "Are you all right?" she asked.

"I'm fine, Mom." The danger was gone now. "Are you two okay?"

"I was afraid," Maya said. "Kai, I tried to protect Mom, but the monster was too big."

"It's okay, Maya, you did a good job. You're both safe now." Kai hugged his little sister and his mom again. It was difficult to let go of them. He had missed them and worried so much.

All around the room, the monsters and mermaids were relaxing. They were talking, now, or dancing to soft music that one of the monsters made using two strings of kelp. Everyone was happy again. It was hard to believe that just moments ago, it had been so tense.

Amphi swam closer, and Delphi came up beside Kai. Delphi gave him the Storm Blaster. He tucked it into his waistband.

"I really am so sorry. But, you haven't seen Poseidon? Truly?"

"No, we haven't seen him."

"That's strange. He's been quiet. Too quiet," Amphi said, pressing her finger to her chin. "But never mind that now. I want to apologize to you. You are all free to go... unless..."

"What?" Delphi asked.

"Would you like to attend a banquet with us? We were going to hold one for Poseidon tonight, but I don't think he will come. It will be my way of apologizing to all of you. Especially to you," Amphi said, nodding to Delphi.

"Why me?" Delphi asked.

"Because you are part mermaid."

Kai and Delphi gasped. Was it true?

Delphi *had* washed up on the beach of Pineapple Cove many years ago. She understood the mer language on the door. She was also a surprisingly good swimmer...

"I can't believe it," Delphi said. "Amphi, Lily, I mean… you lied to us once already."

"I'm telling the truth. You were lost at sea when you were very little, but found by a woman who raised you as her own. The woman's name is Cora," Amphi said.

Delphi nodded. "Wow. I'm really part mermaid?"

Kai's stomach sank. What would this mean for Delphi? She seemed to fit in so well in the Mermaid World. What if she decided to stay?

"Yes. So, will you come to our banquet?" Amphi asked. "Before you go on your way to Pineapple Cove?"

Kai and Delphi looked over at Kai's mom, and she nodded. "All right," they said. "We'll come." Kai's little sister Maya seemed happy about it too. She kept staring around at all the mermaids and monsters, blinking like she still couldn't believe what was happening.

"Oh, but only if you make a promise," Kai said.

"What's that?" Amphi asked.

"Don't send another monster to Pineapple Cove!" Kai announced.

Amphi laughed. "I promise I never will. On my honor. The monsters are my guardians. They do what I ask them to out of love. But I was wrong, and they won't ever harm you again. They are actually very sweet creatures when you get to know them. Isn't that right, Bob?"

Bob blinked his bobble eyes at her, and his jelly lips parted into a toothless smile.

"To the banquet we go," cried Amphi.

CHAPTER 14

SALT SHAKES & PROMISES

The banquet was incredible.

There were all kinds of delicious foods. Sweet candied kelp bursts, and pop-bubble fruits, and delicious crispy seaweed fries. The drinks were even better—underwater salt shakes and upside-down sea-cherry fizzers.

Kai could hardly speak. He was too busy eating. Sammy sat nearby and looked like he was in heaven. He chomped away at his fishy treats, only stopping to nuzzle Delphi.

Delphi was seated next to a young mermaid girl with blue hair. They were happy and chatting non-stop. Delphi fit in here, but Kai secretly hoped she wouldn't stay behind. Aunt Cora would miss her, and he would too.

Heads turned toward the doorway as someone new entered the banquet room.

"Hermes! You made it!" Kai and Delphi ran over and gave him a hug.

"I see you managed just fine without me." Hermes raised an eyebrow at them.

"Long story; we'll tell you about it later," Kai said. Hermes nodded and bowed to Amphi before taking his seat at the table.

Amphi lifted her glass of sea-cherry fizzer. "Attention, everyone. It's time for me to make my announcement."

Everyone around the table, including Bob the sea monster, turned to face Amphi. Apparently, poor Bob was quite clumsy. He had already broken three glasses and twelve plates, and the first chair he'd sat on. That was the real reason he had damaged the shops in Pineapple Cove. He had also ripped the ransom note by accident and forgotten to leave it at Kai's house.

"I want to apologize again to the people of Pineapple Cove. I promise I will never send a monster to your town again. This is the first

and last time. I swear to everyone here, all the
mermaids and humans. I will never ever cause
trouble for Pineapple Cove again. In fact, if you
are ever in need, you can count on our help."

Everyone gave a great cheer as Amphi took
her seat. She drank down her sea-cherry fizzer
and burped. The merpeople laughed. Even Bob
the monster jiggled back and forth in his chair.

Kai frowned. "Wait a second." He raised his hand, politely. "Queen Amphi," he said. "What do you mean the first and the last? This is the second monster that's been to Pineapple Cove."

"Oh my," Amphi said. "I have never sent any monster except for poor old Bob."

Bob the jelly monster waved his goopy arm.

"Only one monster," Kai said. "Then who sent the first one? The giant octopus monster that looked like it was under a spell."

None of them had any idea. It was a question for another day. Today was a day to celebrate.

"Oh yes," Delphi said to the blue-haired mermaid. "I would love to visit some time. In fact, I would love to stay for a while."

Kai's stomach turned over. What if Delphi did decide to stay after all? He wouldn't like that one bit.

The rest of the banquet was spent eating, talking, and laughing. Kai had a merry time joking around with Bob the jelly blob. Kai's mom and little sister listened to the interesting stories that Amphi had to tell. Hermes showed off the chain he broke during his fight with the Collector's guards. He was very proud of it.

"This was wonderful," Kai's mom said. "But I think it's time we go home now."

"Yes, thank you for the banquet, Amphi," Kai said.

"It's the least I could do. I behaved terribly."

Amphi chewed on her bottom lip and twirled a strand of pink around her finger. "And if you do see Poseidon, please tell me. I would like to know where he's been."

"We will," Kai said.

The humans rose around the table, all except for Delphi. She hadn't moved, and her eyes were wide.

"Delphi?" Kai asked. "Are you coming?"

Delphi pressed her lips together. "I was thinking… maybe I should stay. It feels like I belong here. And it's not like Pineapple Cove will miss me."

Kai lowered his gaze. His throat got all tight. "If that's what you want, Delphi, then you should do it. But you belong in Pineapple Cove too. You have Aunt Cora and Captain Hobbs and me."

Sammy barked loudly next to Kai. "And Sammy, of course." Kai looked Delphi in the eye. "If you do come back to Pineapple Cove, I promise I'll focus more on training."

"I promise to show you all my inventions!" shouted Maya.

"And I promise that you will always have a place at our table," said Kai's mom.

"Aarf, aarf!" promised Sammy.

Delphi's eyes glistened. "Thank you...for showing me that Pineapple Cove really is my home." Delphi turned to face Amphi. "I can come back to visit, right?"

"Of course. You can come visit us anytime you want," Amphi said. "Hermes, please take them back through the portal to their home."

"Yes, my Queen," Hermes said, bowing again.

Delphi finally smiled and got up from the table. "Okay, let's go home," she said.

Kai, his mom and sister, Delphi, and Sammy followed Hermes out of the banquet hall. They paired up and rode their sea horses back through Sirenia City. Kai was full of smiles now, and he laughed as his green seahorse did somersaults through the water. The ocean was warm as ever, and when they reached the dock above, it was still daytime. A small sailboat waited for them.

The guards waved goodbye to the group as they sailed back through the magic arch. In a flash, the portal closed, and they continued on toward Pineapple Cove.

Kai and Delphi helped Maya and Kai's mom back toward the shore. They stood on the beach, waving to Hermes, the fading sunlight warm on their faces. Strangely, sunset had only just come.

"I'm so glad to be back," Kai's mom said. "It was very interesting down there, but frightening too."

"I'm tired, Mommy." Maya gave a big yawn. "Can we go home now?"

Kai's mom took Maya's hand, and together, the five of them walked home. Once again, Pineapple Cove was safe.

CHAPTER 15

THE CAPTAIN RETURNS

The next day, Kai and Delphi walked along the sandy beach, talking about all that had happened. Sammy flippered along close behind.

"…and the seahorses were amazing!" Delphi said, doing a little twirl in the sand.

"Yeah! And remember the Collector's palace? And the dancing jellyfish?" Kai replied excitedly.

"Of course!" said Delphi. "We got to explore and face real monsters, just like you wanted."

Kai grinned. "Yeah it was a blast. But I think I'm ready to get back to training now." He frowned, thinking about their missing trainer.

Delphi nodded. "Where do you think Captain Hobbs went? Do you think he's okay?"

Kai shook his head. "I don't know. He said he would be right ba--"

"Aarf! Aarf! Aarf!" Sammy interrupted. He was staring out at the ocean.

"Look!" Delphi pointed at the familiar ship coming towards them.

"It's him! It's Captain Hobbs!" Kai shouted. They ran down to the water and waited for the ship to dock.

Captain Hobbs stood in front of the ship's wheel and waved at them. "Kai, Delphi, you've got to come back with me!" he shouted down to them.

"Where? Why?" Delphi asked.

"It's the crystal egg. I need your help to get it back," the Captain said. "Quick, climb aboard and I'll explain on the way."

Kai and Delphi looked at each other and shrugged. They climbed up the gangplank and onto the ship.

"Where do we start the search?" Kai asked. The ship was still facing Pineapple Cove. "And don't we need to turn the ship toward open waters?"

The Captain smiled with a twinkle in his eye. "Water? Where we're going, we don't need water." Hobbs pulled the wooden lever next to the wheel, and the ship started to shake. The sails above began to expand and inflate. Soon the sky above was blocked out by a giant balloon, decorated in purple and green stripes.

"Whoaaaa!" Kai and Delphi shouted. "This is so cool!"

Sammy covered his eyes with a seal flipper.

The ship rose out of the water and into the sky. It was time for their next adventure.

TO BE CONTINUED.

HIDDEN PINEAPPLE ANSWER KEY

There are 13 pineapples hidden throughout the illustrations in this story. Did you spot them all?

CHAPTER 1 = 🍍

CHAPTER 2 = NONE

CHAPTER 3 = 🍍

CHAPTER 4 = NONE

CHAPTER 5 = 🍍

CHAPTER 6 = 🍍

CHAPTER 7 = 🍍

CHAPTER 8 = 🍍

CHAPTER 9 = 🍍 🍍

CHAPTER 10 = 🍍

CHAPTER 11 = 🍍

CHAPTER 12 = 🍍

CHAPTER 13 = NONE

CHAPTER 14 = 🍍

CHAPTER 15 = 🍍

Hi!

Did you enjoy the story?

I know I did!

If you want to join the team as we go on more adventures, then leave a review!

Otherwise, we won't know if you're up for the next mission. And when we set out on the journey, you may never get to hear about it!

You can leave a review wherever you found the book.

The gang and I are excited to see you on the next adventure!

Hopefully there are snacks . . .

The fantastical adventures of Kai and Delphi in
The Legend of Pineapple Cove

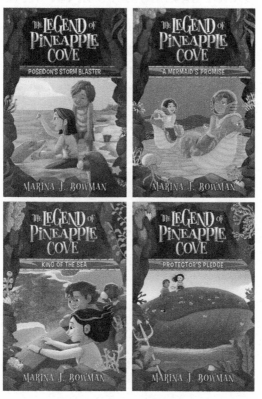

Don't miss Book #3 in the series

King of the Sea

When a powerful crystal egg is stolen, Kai and Delphi journey to Turtle Mountain to get it back. But nothing is as it seems, and the protectors of Pineapple Cove face their biggest challenge yet.

Order now!

thelegendofpineapplecove.com/book2

QUESTIONS FOR DISCUSSION

1. What did you enjoy about this book?
2. What are some of the major themes of this story?
3. How are Kai and Delphi similar? How are they different? How did they help each other in the story?
4. What doubts or fears did the characters express in the book? When have you been afraid? How have you dealt with your fears?
5. The Legend of Pineapple Cove Book #2 ends with some loose ends. What do you think will happen in the next book in the series?

For more Discussion Questions, visit
thelegendofpineapplecove.com/book2

AUNT CORA'S COCO-NUTTY COOKIES

| YIELD: 16 SMALL COOKIES | PREP TIME: 15 MINS |
| COOK TIME: 7 MINS | TOTAL TIME: 25 MINS |

Soft and chewy coconut flour cookies with peanut butter and chocolate, these are a classic Pineapple Cove treat. Make them just like Aunt Cora does for Kai and Delphi!

INGREDIENTS

- 1/2 cup peanut butter
- 2 tablespoons coconut oil
- 1/2 cup brown sugar
- 2 large eggs
- 1 1/2 teaspoons pure vanilla extract
- 1/2 teaspoon baking soda
- 1/4 teaspoon ground cinnamon
- 1/4 teaspoon salt
- 1/2 cup coconut flour
- 1/2 cup chocolate chips

INSTRUCTIONS

1. Preheat the oven to 350 degrees F. Line a cookie sheet with parchment paper or a silicone baking mat.

2. Place the peanut butter, coconut oil, and coconut sugar in a large bowl. Blend together until smooth.

Add the eggs and vanilla and blend again until evenly combined.

3. Sprinkle the baking soda, cinnamon, and salt over the top. Sprinkle in the coconut flour. Blend again until the mixture forms a smooth dough, stopping to scrape the sides of the bowl as needed. Using a spoon or spatula, gently fold in the chocolate chips.

4. With a medium-sized spoon, portion the dough by heaping tablespoons onto the prepared cookie sheet. With your fingers, lightly flatten the dough, as it will not spread during baking.

5. Bake for 7 minutes or until the cookies turn barely golden brown at the edges and feel lightly dry. They will be very soft. Let cool on the baking sheet for 3 minutes, and then transfer the cookies to a wire rack to finish cooling. Repeat with any remaining dough.

6. Enjoy and share with family or friends!

For more recipes, visit

thelegendofpineapplecove.com/book2

ADD YOUR OWN COLOR TO THE MERMAID WORLD!

BRING THIS UNDERWATER SCENE TO LIFE!

For more coloring pages, visit

thelegendofpineapplecove.com/book2

ABOUT THE AUTHOR

MARINA J. BOWMAN is a writer and explorer who travels the world searching for wildly fantastical stories to share with her readers. Ever since she was a child, she has been fascinated with uncovering long lost secrets and chasing the mythical, magical, and supernatural. For her current story, Marina is investigating Pineapple Cove, a mysterious island located somewhere in the Atlantic.

Marina enjoys sailing, flying, and nearly all other forms of transportation. She never strays far from the ocean for long, as it brings her both inspiration and peace. She stays away from the spotlight to maintain privacy and ensure the more unpleasant secrets she uncovers don't catch up with her.

As a matter of survival, Marina nearly always communicates with the public through her representative, Devin Cowick. Ms. Cowick is an entrepreneur who shares Marina's passion for travel and creative storytelling and is the co-founder of Code Pineapple.

Marina's last name is pronounced baʊmən, and rhymes with "now then."

Made in the USA
Monee, IL
31 July 2021